Tale of Magizona

Flairs and Glairs

Publication House

"Tale of Magizona"

ISBN No: " 978-93-90416-78-3"
1st Edition
Language – English and Hindi

Flairs and Glairs
Publication House
Regd. Under MSME Act.

Disclaimer

This is a work of fiction and solely represent the thoughts of the corresponding author of the articles.
Our editors have tried their best to edit the content of all the authors and check the plagiarism.
All the write-ups in this book are unique and are only published in this book.
In case any plagiarism or error is found, only the author is responsible alone, and not the publisher.

Cover Designing and Book Formatting
Shubham Shah

Tale of Magizona

The Battle of Amaris

A. Sai Fhalgun

Abstract

A boy is saved by the celestial beings to fulfill a prophecy. After he is saved and taken to a palace his fate becomes entwined with those of other three chosen to defeat a dark villain and there occurs a series of adventure romance sentiment and fantasy. Will he be able to fulfill the prophecy? Will the oracle be fulfilled?

I dedicate this story to my late grandfather and grandmother
Also, to my father and mother
And all those who have tried to bring me to the field of writing

❖ *I invoke the blessings of Lord Ganesha the remover of obstacles to remove any obstacles that occur while writing this story.*

- ❖ *I invoke the aid of Goddess Sharda or Saraswati the mother of learning, Music, speech. I call upon the wife of Brahma the creator to help me with a continuous flow of imagination throughout my mind.*
- ❖ *I invoke the aid of all the gods in the creation of this story*

Prologue

A woman walked into a barren land and stood there. She closed her almond-like eyes and murmured something with her lips that looked like withered rose petals. As she murmured the wind blew her ebony black hair on her round face. She was wearing a white gown that was flowing with the wind. On her left wrist was a silver bangle bracelet and on her right hand was a silver pearl ring. She completed her murmuring and opened her amber eyes. She pulled out a fist full of powdered ivory from her pouch and blew it in the sky. Soon the ivory settled on the ground and produced a huge white marble palace that gleamed in the sky. Seven stags appeared on the top of the palace facing the center. The lady entered the palace and walked through a secret path into a secret chamber. There she raised a pedestal in front of her. She summoned a bowl and placed it on the center of the pedestal.

She murmured something a pentagram appeared around the bowl. She summoned the elements and nature's magic essence to witness her blood sacrifice. She pulled out a dagger and slashed her wrist producing ten drops of her blood. She then took a lump of clay and built figures of five men and seven women. She then summoned the element of water and mixing her blood drops in it sprayed the water on each figure bringing it to life. As she brought every one of the figures to life, she named them and divided them. Atum, Osiris, and Iris became the judges, Nefertiti, Hana and Tyga became the Executioner's the rest four women became Nymphs and stayed on Earth. She soon with her knowledge of magic and mysticism created a beautiful kingdom.

She was named and crowned as the Great Ancestral Witch Queen Amarya and was placed on the central throne. Once Amarya thought of moving ahead in her studies. She waved her hand and snapped her finger. Soon, her white narrow waist gown turned to a white cloak with a hood that covered her head. Her cat rubbed itself against her. She entered the chamber and snapped her fingers again. Soon, the whole chamber glowed with light. She said looking at her cat "Zelda it's time to raise the champions for my realization of my power and the protection of the kingdom" the cat mewed in approval and relaxed in her place. Amarya went through the chamber until she stopped in front of an image. It was the image of a group of four other people. She started analyzing the portrait when her eyes fell on the description inscribed on the gold plate below

Arachnia, Senora, Jorek, Magicus, Yeta the five late protectors of the realm who sacrificed themselves in the great war.

"The persons of pure will and heart," thought Amarya and went into her robe and pulled out a slim white wand, and waved it drawing a pentagram in the sky. "I call you to form the protection. Spider, Witch Riddler, Illusionist, and the Wizard of Ice come out of the graves and defend my kingdom". As her spell completed there appeared in front of her the five champions.

Arachnia was a beautiful woman with a tall and slim figure. Her eyes were black with curved eyebrows. Her hair was black and tied into a tight bun with a spider pin in it. She wore a brown silk gown with hanging down full sleeves. Her fingers were as slender as reeds. In her right hand, she wore a silver spider ring. Senora was next. She was beautiful in a golden fan collar gown and a golden ivy circlet on her brown hair. Her eyes were brown and her eyebrows were angled. She looked quite beautiful with a ruby ring.

Magicus wore a tail-coat and top hat with a black topaz ring. He had cropped hair and neatly trimmed beard and looked quite charming. Jorek wore a black suit-pant with a white shirt and a monocle. His hair was cropped and had a confused look at his hawk-like face. Yeta was a handsome young man with silver hair neatly cropped and a clean-shaven face and wore a grey cloak and had his wolf by his side.

"Lady Amarya why did you bring the five champions here what is thy wish," asked Arachnia "I want to realize the full potential of light magic to save my friends," said Amarya "I see so you want us to teach you to reach the highest point of light magic. Then for that, you must impress us with your extent" said Senora, and to show her strength she twisted her hand and telekinetically broke the neck of a soldier spying on them. "I will try my level best, Masters," She said, and using her little knowledge of magic created five statues of the five.

So, thus began the training of the White Witch by the Champions. Arachnia taught her the detection of Shadow Magic, Witchcraft and Potion craft, Senora strengthened her telekinesis and telepathic skills, Magicus taught her spells, Jorek taught her Illusionism, and Yeta taught her Ice kinesis.

Yeta was a good friend to Jorek so he took him to a side and conveyed something in his ears "What! Are you insane? When did you feel like this for your student" said Jorek "I don't know from the day she summoned us from the portrait I gave away my heart to her" said Yeta "But you know that there is a great difference between the two of you? She is a mortal witch and you are an immortal spirit. To be one you would have to enter a mortal coil and give up your immortality" said Jorek " No need for that, I just decided to share my immortality with Amarya as a gift of my love" said Yeta "But to do that you will have to do the ritual and get a human body" said Jorek " I just have it" said Yeta eyeing the statue that Amarya created for them to stay.

 Yeta narrated everything to the others and asked for their help. Magicus agreed and went to the statue. He started murmuring a spell and made the sign of a double helix "I need the soul of a person to balance the scale of life and death" said Magicus. Arachnia twisted her hand and dematerialized into a cloud of black smoke.

She appeared in the castle of Zakura while he was sleeping and using her magic, she killed one of his soldiers and re-dematerialized with his body and rematerialized at the chamber. Magicus placed the body in front and chanted verse. Soon, the evil soldier turned to dust and his evil appeared as a black orb. Magicus used the pure rays of the sun and destroyed the darkness. Soon, Yeta's soul got absorbed into the statue and his soul form became the form of his real self "But how will you take her test in this mortal shell" asked Senora "Don't worry he now can leave his body but only for a few hours" said Magicus and they renamed Yeta Irvin.

The next day her test began and Amarya excelled in all the tests of the four champions. Now It was Yeta's turn and using the power gifted by Magicus he took Amarya's test and she excelled that to "Amarya you have excelled in all our tests and have earned the full powers of a Sorceress. Therefore, we the champions bestow you the title of Ancient Tribunal Sorceress the Queen of the Good and Slayer of the wicked" as the Champions uttered these words Amarya's dress changed in a cloud of golden cloud. Now she was in a white narrow waist gown with a fan collar and stout fur cuffs.

 On her wrist appeared a bracelet bangle made of gold with an ancient inscription. Around her neck was a silver choker with a central ruby and around her head was a silver circlet. The Masters motioned for Yeta to now reveal his feelings to her. Yeta held the hand of Amarya and said "Amarya, from the day you summoned the champions from the portrait and displayed your strength and magic. I developed feelings for you. Therefore In front of the masters and Nature's power, I confess that I love you and ask you do you feel the same" Amarya was taken aback and was quite happy with this proposal but had a doubt "My Lord I do feel the same for you but I fear that you may lose me due to the ending of this mortal shell and I cannot dare to break your heart" said Amarya remorsefully

"Amarya there is a solution for that, I have something that I made for the both of you and Yeta has completed the ritual of his sacrificing his immortality and now he will be a half-mortal and so would you," said Magicus and Senora. Senora brought a goblet of a pink liquid and asked them both to drink it from the same goblet. As Magicus recited a magic verse half of Yeta's immortality entered that of Amarya and Yeta returned into his human body "From Now on you are Lord Irvine and Lady Amarya".

For a few long years, Amarya lived with her husband and they ruled happily but then came the darkest and most terrible night of all, for it was the night of betrayal and massacre. Zakura was the advisor to the kingdom who was one of the creations of Amarya but he was quite obsessed with dark arts and decided to opt it. The Dark Magic appeared in front of him as a skeleton in a cloak with a scythe and offered to make him stronger than his king and queen. Zakura was asked to sacrifice the lives of twenty-two people of pure heart and soul on the eclipse.

Zakura killed the king with an ancient weapon that broke immortal ties and similarly others on the time When the people were celebrating the Festival of Dayorus or the Festival of Pure Souls. He killed twenty-one pilots and was after the Queen but was injured and banished from The Land of Wisdom forever by the Queen, the pure souls, and the nine protectors. Zakura landed in the same place where he summoned Dark Magic and sacrificed the hearts, he collected from the twenty-one people and poured the crushed ashes at his foot. When the Magic asked for the last heart, he used his hypnosis and summoned a pure-hearted man who was not of the royal blood but was the heart of a noble warrior clan and killed him.

This made the White Magic appear as a Silver Gatekeeper and curse him to die in the hands of the same noble-hearted pure soul human raised by the hands of his doom. He was thrown into the darkest of pits where he established the Kingdom of Darkura. The White Witch Queen of the Land of Wisdom was promised by the Witch that her tears will not be shed in vain and Zakura would soon perish. Then White magic blessed her with immense powers and asked her to protect the kingdom. Amarya waved her hand over her palace and turned it invisible with protective charms and spells. From then on, she was waiting for the boy prophesied.

After a few years, at the time when the prophecy was to be fulfilled

The sunlight was filling the sky and earth with its brightness. The birds were chirping creating a symphony merged with the sounds of the animals. Everything was peaceful and in a mood of celebration. It seemed as if there was a soothing celebration that was attracting celestial beings to the forest on the island of Nymphora. Soon, a lady in orange fire gown walked into the forest, her hair was red as fire, her eyes were amber and eyebrows were arched. her ears were pointed and her nose was straight. Around her neck was a necklace of rubies, a ruby bracelet rested on her wrist,

 a large ruby ring gleamed on her right-hand ring finger. Her smile was as warm as a bonfire. A pair of macaws was sitting on a tree of which the male told his mate "here comes Furia the nymph who can control the element of fire" To which the mate gave a call of surprise.

Furia went to the nearby stream and closed her eyes focusing her concentration on something. Soon, the water took the shape of a lady with black hair adorned with a coral crown. The woman had azure blue eyes and straight eyebrows. Her ears were also pointed like those of Furia and her nose was straight. She wore a sea blue gown with a brooch in the shape of a conch shining on her breast. She was as peaceful as the ocean "Welcome Darya I am waiting for you; Come out we have to gather the others" said Furia as excited as a flame.

Darya and Furia went throughout the forest calling out Aspen. Soon, a melodious voice was heard in response. As they followed it, they found Aspen sitting under a tree playing flute and surrounded by the whole forest fauna. She was equally beautiful like her sisters for she resembled them in most of the facial features except eyes which were brown and had brown hair. She wore a gown made of the bark of dead trees and dried leaves. An ivy bracelet adorned her wrist and an ivy circlet adorned her hair. She wore a pair of rudraksha as earrings. Even her smile could bring life to nature.

As the trio of nymphs were exchanging pleasantries a massive storm appeared accompanied by lightening "Thora calm down" shouted Aspen and soon the storm settled taking the form of a beautiful lady with silver hair, rounded eyebrows, and smile like the winds of spring. The four Nymphs hugged each other and were talking happily when suddenly Furia stopped talking and closed her eyes feeling something. Soon, her voice entered into a trance-like state "The child is about to be born. The one who would bring the doom of darkness, who will light the flame of rebellion to ward off the darkness of evil monarchy is going to be born. The lioness will give birth to the cub" said Furia and snapped her fingers turning themselves to midwives. "Thora Aspen moves into the east direction where you will find a warrior queen being safely transferred in a caravan bring her here," said Furia.

Thora and Aspen did as they were told and saw the caravan that carried the queen. Thora took a fistful of dust and casting a spell created a massive storm from it making the caravan stop and the people run away. As the coast cleared Thora settled the storm. Aspen went to the back of the caravan and found the queen with her sword beside her. Aspen quickly took some dust and sprinkled it on the queen making her sleep. Then Thora and Aspen carried the queen to the cottage made by Furia and Darya.

After a struggling night, the child was born but with a heavy price of the life of his mother. The nymphs started taking care of the child but soon, they knew they had to face the evil. Zakura was an evil ruthless cunning and cruel king who ruled the kingdom of Darbola. He was an invader who was a pest in the land of Magizona. Zakura was a tall well-built figure with sunken eyes. He wore a black feather-trimmed cape. Once while he was discussing something his soldiers brought in a tall young man with them. After his discussion was over, they threw the young man at his feet

"My Lord while we were plundering a village as per your direction This young man tried to stop us". Zakura closed his eyes for a moment "How exactly did he do it" asked Zakura, the soldiers said "He screamed at us and abused us. He even killed the commander in chief with a single punch" "Oh a headstrong boy with super strength, is he?" said Zakura and clapped three times.

A soldier walked in "Bring the potion in for this special guest of mine" he ordered the soldier. The soldier ran out and brought a small cup of a green-colored liquid "This is a token of appreciation for your bravery" said Zakura so nicely that the young man gave in and drank the potion. After a moment he felt a burning sensation in his throat and spoke but could only talk in a shrill voice "What is this sensation?" "Oh, don't worry those are your vocal cords burning" As the young man tried to scream, he found he lost his voice. Zakura then walked to him and gave him a tight slap so strong that he fell to the ground "Take him to the prison tower and began the process of making him, my servant. I want him here by midday"

the soldiers dragged the man to the prison tower. This was Zakura's cruelty but he feared his upcoming fate. After four days of the birth of the child, Zakura got the news from his spies and fumed with rage. He decided to kill the baby that very night.

Zakura attacked the nymphs by blending into the Darkness but had to die due to the magical powers of the Nymphs. The Nymphs grew concerned about the child's safety. They soon used their telepathy and asked the Tribunal to protect the child and the prophecy. Soon three hooded people appeared in front of the Nymphs who gave them the baby and sent them away.

The hooded figures were none other than Atum, Riana, and Osiris the three judiciaries of the Tribunal which was created by Amarya. They returned to the land with the baby. As they entered the throne room sitting on the top of the triangularly arranged thrones was Amarya with her cat in her lap the cat jumped from Amarya's lap and going down the path of stairs that began from her throne and divided the triangle with the queen descending the stairs majestically "Excellent Riana you have protected the prophecy. Now take him in" she said to Riana who took the child into the queen's chamber and laid him in the cradle. The queen entered the room and started swinging the cradle making the child sleep. Slowly she raised him with her elder son who was born before the king died.

The Masters taught him mystic arts and the power of magic with its laws and discipline. The protectors taught him warfare and the judiciary took the laws and rules of the Land of Wisdom. Thus, eighteen years passed in her raising him into a fearless handsome lad. Leonor was now eighteen years old. He was tall and well-built with short black hair and round ears, a handsome beardless facial feature, and a kind and polite nature. When Arom was eligible to rule she did not hide anything from them including how Leonor came to her and where his father was and the betrayal of Zakura to them. When both the princes were asked about their wish to rule the kingdom. Leonor himself gave up his claim to the throne and decided to spend his life in the library and become a storyteller and healer as if he understood the disputes and riots it will cause and the questions which will raise on his parentage. Therefore, Arom was placed on the Throne of King Irvinus and Leonor became his advisor and the head of Protectors.

. But Zakura feared his death and therefore in his fear and the craving to wipe out the entire Kingdom but little did he know that he was being watched by Amarya through her mirror. Amarya called her adopted son and told him to find the three people with the symbol of Raasi Chakra on their wrists and to bring them to a place she tells him when he finds them. Thus, equipped with the knowledge of magic, combat, and weaponry and carrying a sword and a dagger her son went through a secret portal to the City of Hope where he would find the Trio Guardians. After sending him away Amarya stepped into her mirror for mediation till the time of the arrival of the Chosen.

Chapter -1

Anubis was chasing a deer when suddenly in between they appeared a young boy laughing "Who are you?" asked the prince "If you want to know who I am then Find me" said the young boy with a laugh and dematerialized into a blue cloud. The prince started searching for the boy when suddenly he felt a burning on his right hand. As she pulled back his sleeve, he saw a circle with a roaring lion appearing on his wrist. He decided to go to the back of the boy and find out. Anubis was the Prince of the City of Hope. He was a young man with short black hair and hazel eyes. He was a tall well-built person with round ears and a straight nose and a stubble on his cheeks. Anubis thought for a few minutes and searched for the boy.

A young girl with black eyes and elven ears sat outside her cottage and was grinding herbs when the same boy appeared to her " Mix a little water and turmeric it might be successful" said the boy "Who are you boy where did you come from how do you know so much about Herbology "Find me and seek your answers" said the boy and dematerialized into a blue cloud. The young girl sat on the floor of the cottage and was thinking when a call came from inside "Kiara why is it taking so much time?" "Coming Father, "said Kiara tying her brown hair into a messy bun and taking the mortar and pestle went back to her cottage.

Tien was working in the armory and was beating the iron when the boy appeared and advised "You have beaten the iron enough don't put your anger on your master in your work" Who are you kid? Go back to your house, the armory is not the place for kids" said Tien. He was an apprentice to a blacksmith from a young age. He had tanned skin and black eyes. His hair was shorter and his ears were round and beardless face. He wore a sleeveless leather tunic and trousers. "I am here for you, as for who I am? Find me and get the answer yourself" said the boy and turned into a blue cloud. Tien thought about this for a moment till his master came and checked his work and appreciated him and asked his forgiveness to pressure him in his work.

In the evening, Anubis told his guards that he will be out for a few days and will return soon and donning his quiver full of arrows and his bow and wearing a hooded cloak rode in the search for the boy. Kiara wore a green gown and hanging a bag full of medicines and poison and taking a sickle in her other hand She moved to find the boy. Tien wore a leather cloak and taking the hammer he used to beat the iron went in search of the boy.

As destiny would have it the three met at the same place. They saw a hooded man drawing something on the ground "I see you have come to seek the answer to the vision and to know who I am" said the man and he rose. All three of them see the man turn at them armed themselves with their respective weapons. The hooded man waved his hand and made all the weapons vanishing. "I am Leonor The Member of Castle Amaris of the Land of Wisdom and am searching for the people with the symbol of Raasi Chakra which you three have on your wrist. And as he spoke Kiara and Tien checked their wrists and saw the burned mark of the scorpion and bull. "You three are chosen for a purpose and it's time for you three to come with me to the Land of Wisdom to know your destiny. But before that I saw you playing with toy weapons now, I need to check your real capabilities in arms and spells "said Leonor and making a symbol in the air he summoned the magic spell and created a portal for them.

As they exited the portal each was wearing iron tunic and leather trousers and a cape was hanging from their back. Leonor waved his hand and summoned their weapons. Kiara was given a sword, Anubis bow and arrow, and Tien a

Warhammer. Leonor asked them to attack him. First Kiara attacked him with slash and thrust but failed and was knocked out by him using telekinesis. Next, it was Anubis who constantly fired arrows at him but Leonor with a single wave of his hand broke all the arrows in two as if they were just twigs.

Last came Tien with his hammer but Leonor dodged it clearly and with a single push threw him at his back. Now the three came together but he disappeared from his place and made them fall "Excellent I am impressed. You have done excellently. We will improve them more so you can find entrance into my brother's kingdom" said Leonor and spinning his hand created a blue cloud twister dematerializing everyone with him.

They all rematerialized at a battle arena "Don't worry this is all just a setup by me to train you all to become the warriors. He began training the three. After three months, they became true warriors and he narrated to them why he searched for them and what is going to happen.

He again teleported them and himself in the form of blue cloud and rematerialized them at his palace "This is Amaris kingdom of King Arom and the Ancestor Amarya. You will be tested through the gates of the palace protected by the great protectors. Good luck" he said and dematerialized into a blue cloud. He came back into Amarya's chamber and waving his hand on the mirror said: "Mirror Show me my Mother" the mirror rippled and soon appeared the image of Amarya meditating in her world " Mother" he called soon Amarya opened her eyes and stood on her legs " Son, Did you bring them" she said " Yes" he replied. Amarya walked out of the mirror and touching the stubble cheeks of her son she kissed him on his forehead "Then it's time they must be tested" said Amarya and summoned the three warriors "Go and test the arriving guests" the three warriors disappeared.

Kiara stepped in front and touched the door and dematerialized into a golden dust cloud. She was materialized she saw herself in a small battle arena and was dazed. "Welcome," said Nefertiti. She was a beautiful young woman with black hair tied into a ponytail. Her eyes were green and her eyebrows were arched. From her ears hung emerald sapphire earrings and on her right ear was a peacock shaped ear cuff. She wore gown weaved from solid metal gold. In her right hand, she held a lance "I am the Phoenix" she said and attacked Kiara who gave her a tough fight. In end she managed a pleasant victory

"I am impressed, You and your friends may pass" said Nefriti and disappeared.

Kiara returned smiling to her friends and they passed the gate. On the next door, Anubis went to the door and touched it. Soon, he dematerialized into a maroon cloud of dust. As he materialized, he found in front of him a hulking figure in sleeveless black leather tunic "I am Aleser the tiger let's dance" said the warrior and fought with Anubis after a heavy duel Anubis defeated the warrior "You have been groomed well. I am happy to lose in the hands of trained warrior" said Aleser and disappeared opening the second gate. The last gate was for Tien who fought with a warrior who disappeared into thin air to fight him.

Tien calculated his move and as the warrior appeared he kicked the ground bringing out large rock and kicked it at the warrior who slashed it with a single slash from his lessen fan but was defeated with a single kick from Tien " You are worthy, please enter" said the warrior opening the final gate to the palace. After entering through the final gate, they arrived at the palace and met the queen who had just left the mirror and the ruler Arom who was hugging his brother with love and warmth. "Son take them to their chambers," said Amarya "Sure mother, "said Leonor but secretly whispered to his friends "I have a small secret to share come with me," he said escorting them.

Leonor took the three champions through a pair of massive iron and oak doors into the royal library "My group called the Secret Keepers, under whom we are constructing a small secret army" said Leonor. "So, you are the Triguardians," asked a woman politely. Her hair was black and curly. Her blue eyes shined with bravery and her angled brows made her beautiful, her ears were pointed. She wore a cowboy hat and a full-sleeved purple gown with trousers and high heels "Guys this is Aleena" said Leonor introducing the witch who shook Kiara's hands with her leather gloves "This is Medusa" he said pointing at the other lady. This woman had straight hair with green eyes and s-shaped eyebrows. She wore a gown with a fan collar and held a snake staff in her hand.

 "This is Zorek," said Leonor pointing at the young man of his age. Zorek had a neatly cropped hair and a trimmed beard. His eyes were brown and his nose was slightly hooked. He wore brown tunic and trousers with an eagle feather-trimmed overcoat. "This is Moris my best friend," he said introducing the other man standing in a corner. Moris was tall and well built. His brown hair was in a crew cut and his face was beardless. His eyes were black. A medallion of amethyst hung from his neck and an amethyst ring adorned his right-hand finger.

"Where is Cynthia?" Leonor asked Athena "I don't know," she said. Leonor called out to Cynthia and soon a white cloud appeared in front of him and there was a woman with silver hair and pale skin with silver eyes and an ice circlet. She was lightly adorned with silver jewelry on her hands and neck which resembled ice " This is Cynthia Witch of Ice and water and Queen of Aurobog kingdom of white Witches" She greeted them and pulled out her thin wand from her gown held it completely in the palm of her hand and gave a graceful bow.

Leonor again called out Nomak and a cloud of brown dust appeared revealing a young man with a neatly trimmed beard and shaggy hair wearing a brown tunic "Guys this is lord Nomak the lord of Western Mountains and another one of my able sorcerers" "It's nice to meet all of your secret society members but we would like to know about your army". "Our army will be used for the upcoming battle with Zakura. It consists of all those young warriors who have a brave heart and enthusiasm to do something for the kingdom in which they live. Some are children completing their studies whereas the others are monk students from the monasteries after their training. They are trained in most of the sorceries, mystic skill, element manipulation, and other stuff" said Leonor "and this is done under the secret orders of the King and the queen mother" said Arom who just entered

Chapter - 2

Amarya called the Guardians the next morning and asked them to display the things they learned to her during combat "As you wish my lady" they said and got ready with the weapons they knew. Amarya snapped both her hand fingers and changed into an outfit with full sleeve gown and pointed collars and a double ring chain adorned her hand "First I choose you Anubis as you are the leader then I shall fight with you two Kiara and Tien together" she explained and got ready to attack.

Anubis summoned his inner power and accessed his Rashi Chakra and summoned Leo. As he started fighting Amarya dodged his moves for a few minutes but jumped up and coming down stood on one foot raising the other behind her gracefully and holding a tessen fan in her hand "You have a lot of heat and ferocious nature of a lion but that won't work. I was not the only one to create the three Generals I also trained them in every way of a warrior" and she started slashing and cutting him with the fan while still standing on one foot. Then she gave him a final slash and sent him flying backward and hiding her face partially behind the fan started smiling.

Then she called Kiara and Tien. Kiara summoned her Scorpio and started punching and wrist hitting and finally joining the two fingers of her right hand used it as a scorpion sting but Amarya jumped out of her way and with a huge pressure punched her with an open palm and at last creating an azure blue bolt fired it hitting Kiara square in the chest and sending her beside Anubis. Tien was the last who accessed his inner Taurus but was also no match for Amarya. She dodged his rock slides jumped high in the sky when he created an earthquake by stomping the ground and finally fought him by staying in the air. In the end, she turned back, and standing, on one hand, kicked him in the chest so hard that he almost broke the wall of the fort.

"The three of you need to train a bit more. I am impressed with your skill but you give up easily and refuse to notice the strength and weakness of the enemy. You did not try to watch my moves clearly and thought you are the only mightiest of all the people If you continue doing this mistake it will become a glitch for your enemy to win and Zakura is not only powerful but also ruthless. He will hang your corpses on the gates of his kingdom if you don't defeat him" She said calmly as if none of this is a big issue "From tomorrow onwards I shall take your lessons and make you be prepared for your war" she said and walked away "She is strong and intelligent. A beauty with brains. No wonder she is ruling the kingdom these past years with a strong hand and kind heart. A rare quality for a woman of her age" said Anubis rubbing the pain in his shoulder

"She used that fan as if it was her wing those shielding, slashing, cutting were highly expertise and graceful, if she gets into a war than surely her opponents will lose their heads on her sword skills just as we licked dust in front of her fan skills. She is a warrior in true nature" said Kiara "Well whatever she is it is glad that from tomorrow she would take our training. Now let us go I am getting restless" said Tien laughing and slapping Anubis on his shoulder which made him laugh as well and they both went to their chamber with Kiara smiling and following them.

Morris went to his office in the castle and started rummaging through the shelves until he found the leather-bound book. He opened the buckle of the book and went through the pages until he found an important line which attracted his focus

Moris got happy and quickly wrote the inscription down in a parchment paper and then running to his crystal ball he rubbed it softly hissing "Show me, King Sylvan, now". Soon the ball started clouding and there appeared the image of a frail old man wearing an overcoat and a crown his face was wrinkled and thin but his voice was as strong as iron. His hair was thinning and his nose was hooked with human-like ears "Lord Sylvan today I have a favor to get from you and will soon get your help in this purpose" said Moris but suddenly fell into a thinking "Whom shall I give this weapon too. Leonor, Arom, Kiara, Anubis, Tien and everyone else has his weapon either as a spell or an item" then suddenly his mind gave an idea " I shall give this gift to the person who will be able to lift it" said Moris and searched his books for a spell and found it "Yes this would help me in locating the one who can wield this weapon for the final war" said Moris and sat down to scribble and design the shape of the weapon. Finally, after he was satisfied, he sat down to think about how to find the person who can help him in finding the scroll and finally decided to ask for Leonor's help.

"Thank you, Mother, for taking care of the Guardians training with your help they will surely be skilled to fight anyone," said Leonor when his mother told him about the days incident "Don't thank me, son. I just went a mile forward with your duty" said Amarya when suddenly the chamber doors opened and Moris entered in his trench coat and trousers "Good morning my Lady" said Moris "Good morning Moris, why have you come here? Is everything all right?" asked Amarya "Everything is good my lady I just want to have a private conversation with Leonor for a secret weapon I am building. So, can I borrow him" he said "Sure why not whatever you do is a contribution to the war, go ahead," said Amarya. Moris quickly grabbed Leonor's hand and pulled him to his chamber.

As they went into Moris chamber he closed the doors and turning to Leonor he said "Friend I need your help. King Sylvan has a secret scroll that can energize the weapon I am going to forge. Therefore, Leonor you must acquire the scroll and keep the king safe and alive" said Moris "Sure Moris as a close friend I will help you. I am going to save the king and bring the scroll to you but you could have told this in front of Mother" said Leonor "I could not risk telling this to anyone till the weapon is made and the chosen is found" said Moris " Got it, Now I shall disguise myself and go to King Sylvan" said Leonor and waved his hand. Soon, he was covered in a blanket and dematerialized into a cloud of blue smoke.

He rematerialized secretly behind the audience and covering himself with the blanket as a poor man entered the crowd. "His Majesty! King Sylvan the Lord of The Mystic Realm and the Guardian of the Ultimate Secret" announced the announcer from the dais which was followed by an uproar from the audience. Leonor went through the audience and stood in the center watching the king give his speech. Soon, he noticed some other person moving near the king with a dagger.

 As Leonor focused his vision on the dagger held hand his eyes glowed blue and the metal started heating till the person dropped it and screamed out in pain attracting the attention of the whole crowd. As he was about to run Leonor gave a wave of his hand sprouting ivy from the ground and tied the man in his place.

The King was astounded by the talent of the young man in a blanket and told his minister to summon the man. "Who are you?" "I am Aragog a messenger of Lord Leonor. I have been sent here to gather the mystic knowledge to energize his weapon" said Leonor and the king believed him for Leonor was in a glamour spell. He clapped his hands and a soldier came running "Adjourn the gathering" the soldier ran to the announcer and conveyed it to him "The public addressing is adjourned for today" said the announcer.

The King took Aragog to a secret door and pulling out his stone locket placed it in the gap. The doorknob turned itself and the gate opened. As they entered, they saw a scroll roll hanging in midair. The king opened his hand and the scroll came flying to him " Here it is, take it to your Lord and tell him that I am grateful to him and from now on I am an ally to the kingdom of Amaris" said the King " My Lord but I don't think you should stay here" said Aragog and created a twister cloud of blue dust around them both and dematerialized into it.

As the King opened his eyes, he found himself in the library of Amaris "Where are we" he asked "In my palace" said Leonor and surprised the king by making the glamour spell wear off "You are Leonor. So, you tricked me" said the king angrily "No I did not trick you. I just did not want your people to know or their life would have been in danger. If I would have come in my true form Zakura would have known and abducted both of us for the sake of his pleasure and I couldn't risk losing you Lord Sylvan" and Leonor's explanation worked on him " Now I will send you back with no memory of meeting me or the existence of the scroll but only being my ally" said Leonor and placed his hand on Sylvan's forehead as he murmured. Then Leonor took away the memories in the form of blue smoke which he transferred to his vial. Then Leonor sent the King away back to his kingdom.

Moris and Leonor worked for three days and three nights and forged the weapon in the form of chakra. Then Moris took a vial of fairy dust and his spell book and sprinkling the dust caused it to weigh more than it should be " Now except for the chosen one this will not be lifted by any person" said Moris and gestured Leonor to lift it which he couldn't and after a smile, he turned to Moris " Moris soon a new kind of army will merge with us. They will be quite powerful therefore after the final war they will have to be taken to the unknown and inaccessible place where no one would find them by the two guardians. Therefore, I require you to write a letter to our allies in the north to send secret Guards to us when we reach the final day of war" said Leonor to which Moris nodded and ran off to write the letter.

The next morning a letter was sent to the so-called allies in the Northern Secret Society also called the Magna Eye who was responsible for the sealing protection of the underworld gate and always was ready for any kind of help asked by Leonor. In his letter to the Magna Eye, he wrote

Dear Ally

We are going to require your help for the final battle against Zakura and his army and would require secret protectors for an important task of taking the most powerful creatures after the war to a secret hideout. On the fifth day when the moon is full send three of your spies to the Western Sea Shore and ask them to wait for us and meet us secretly with only one of them revealing his whereabouts and they should come at different times so that no one knows what we are doing. This final battle will be a tough one So we ask you that after providing the spies you and your society should go into hiding and break off your connection publicly with them but secretly talking to them

Moris

The lady who got the letter understood and called three hooded figures and told them " I just got a letter from Lord Leonor's friend Moris requesting our assistance in an important task and has asked me to send my best people therefore on the fifth day when the moon is full you shall travel to the Western Sea Shore and meet Moris secretly with only one of you telling your address to him" she said and sent them away. She was a beautiful woman with golden hair and wore a gold fan collared gown with an eye-shaped ring. She was the head of the Magna Eye and was called Cecilia.

Chapter – 3

Amarya for three days took the Guardians training and taught them spells and magic with Leonor now taking the special lesson of studying the aura signatures of people with a spell. Soon they were excelling in weaponry mystic arts and other skills and started they excelled even in their tests of strength, knowledge, and valor and impressed everyone.

The very next day, Leonor called Anubis, Kiara, and Tien "Now it is time you receive your power cores. Go to the realm of Erismir, meet Lord Mordred, and find the lady Shayra. You will get to know her by the presence of her aura which you will feel once you meet her. Shayra is the only person who can take you to your power cores." said Leonor and casting a spell created a portal through which he made them go by reminding them "Remember the ways I taught you to study aura signatures". They went into the portal which opened to the other realm the kingdom of Erismir.

Erismir was a vast kingdom ruled by the just king Mordred. The city had houses made of gold and bricks. Erismir was situated in a vast jungle with some trees having the ability to talk and walk. This realm was different from other realms for it housed the fairies. Anubis and the others went to the fort which was neat and clean but due to many wars had many scars that gave it a gothic appearance which was enhanced with creeping climbing ivies.

The door was huge and made up of wood with iron nails studded in it and a giant eye with an ostrich egg-sized ruby peaked on them. A guard opened the gate a little and asked the Guardians "What business do you have here?" We came here to meet Lord Mordred; we are his highly important guests".

Mordred hugged them and asked them to sit "Lord Mordred we are not here to talk to you but rather we are here to meet the orphan girl you took as a serving wench. May we meet her" said Anubis "Sure, let me call her," said Mordred and screamed "Layla! Layla!" a girl wearing a rough spun gown appeared her eyes were purple and her ears were pointed. Her smile was enough to give life to millions of trees "We would like to test the aura in her" said Tien and gestured at Kiara.

Kiara held Layla's hand and closed her eyes and started sensing something. After a few minutes of murmuring a spell, Kiara left her hand and told the others "It is her. It's Shayra"

Anubis quickly turned to Mordred and said " You are quite lucky for you got the Gatekeeper to work for you" " I don't know what you are talking about," said Mordred " This is not Layla a wench but it's Shayra the queen and the only person who can take us to our power cores," said Anubis

 "That is why you came here for the Gatekeeper, sure you can take her now or later," said Mordred to which Anubis thanked him and hugged him with a friendly warm gesture but little did they knew that they were being watched by a spy of Zakura. Layla quickly ran out and seeing the birds fly pulled a dagger from her sleeve and threw it at the bird which slashed the bird's wing and crippled it but the bird managed to fly near the entrance of the underworld and crawled into it.

"We need to move now" Layla cried pulling out her belongings and stashing them in her bag and she asked them to follow her she closed her eyes and turned back into Shayra with elven ears and eagle eyes angled brows and a straight nose the purple in her eyes and the auburn color of her hair gave her a much more beautiful and fierce look. Around her neck, she wore an amethyst pendant and a ruby ring on her finger. Her tall stature impressed even the people who claimed they did not love As She turned back to Shayra Mordred bowed in front of her " I am honored to see the daughter who came to my doorstep helplessly as a Gatekeeper, I am ashamed that you had to work as a servant in my home please forgive me" said Mordred " No Lord Mordred It is I who was honored to act as your daughter and please don't ask for forgiveness, you just believed that I was an orphan and took me under your wing. You need not be ashamed of yourself" said Shayra.

 Zakura was in his castle discussing his plans when a man limped through the entrance crying with pain and trying to block the bleeding "What happened? Who did this to you?" asked Zakura "A which disguised as a serving wench, she did this to me by throwing a dagger at me. But I managed to escape with a little secret which cost me this wound" said the man

"What is that secret?" asked Zakura " The witch is called Shayra and she is a Gatekeeper who is protecting the Guardians power cores," said the man " Excellent," said Zakura and waving his hand over the wound he cured it to a mere scratch and walked to the center " Diavon !" he shouted and a man wearing an iron armor and helm walked to him "Yes master," said the monster with his one good eye peering at Zakura " I want you to capture the woman named Shayra and bring her to me. Kill anyone who dare come in your way" said Zakura and sent him off to the castle of Mordred with a batch of soldiers.

Shayra quickly explained "Now I shall take you all through a magic door to my land from where we shall gather an ally and move further in the quest," said Shayra. Suddenly there was a pound on the door "Quick hide" said Mordred to the group and opened a secret chamber " There is a secret door just on the other side of this chamber run away from there after I distract the guards" said Mordred and ran to open the door "Who are you people?" he asked the soldiers " We are Zakura's men and are searching for a sorceress, where is she?" said Diavon.

 Mordred burst out laughing "Sorry for the laughter, but how can you people think that I will harbor a sorceress?" asked Mordred "That is not our concern, tell us where is your serving wench?" asked Diavon "But Why? She has taken leave for she is ill" said Mordred but Diavon ignored him and ordered his soldiers to search every corner "You should know that you cannot search my house without permission" shouted Mordred so loud that Shayra and the Guardians were alerted.

They quickly ran to the other door and escaped into the forest. Every soldier returned with a negative result making Diavon suspicious till his eye fell on the locked door "Open it" he said but Mordred refused and started twisting his wrist creating a spell. Even after much pressure Mordred refused and attacked the guards with magic bolts. Diavon quickly reacted and stabbed the good king in his stomach. Diavon entered the chamber and found the trap door open. He returned and lifting the half-dead king demanded the address and got none as

As they reached the end of the forest Shayra turned back and let out a scream of disbelief, horror, and sadness as Mordred's castle engulfed in flames and started running towards it " Wait Shayra you are flowing into emotions and forgetting your duty" said Anubis " The one who helped me by keeping me under his wing is burning in those flames and I don't know if he is dead or alive, what sense of duty is important than that" said Shayra her eyes red with tears " I know he is a father to you, he sacrificed himself so that you can fulfill your duty as a Gatekeeper. You can pay off his debts by fulfilling your duty and vanquishing the evil Zakura" said Kiara "You are right, Zakura is responsible for this and he will surely pay it. I curse him that he will miss his target during the end of the Final battle" said Shayra and ran with everyone into the forest.

As they reached the ending there standing in front of them was Diavon. Shayra and the others thought of running back but we're surrounded "Poor Mordred, thought he could fool us by letting you escape through the trap door and distract us. Now he died and burned" said Diavon enough to make Shayra glare at him furiously " Oh the little princess is angrily glaring at me…Oh I am so scared" mocked Diavon but soon his mocking laugh turned into a dreadful wail as he started feeling burns and slowly started burning with a burst of flames and turned to ashes. Shayra used this as a distraction and ran away into the forest. five soldiers ran at their back giving them a close chase. Shayra stopped in mid tracks and closed her eyes. As she opened them, they glowed, she cupped her hands around her mouth and howled. As her eyes turned normal, she persuaded the Guardians to run with her. Soon a pack of wolves came out of nowhere and attacked the chasing soldiers and tore them apart while Shayra smiled from the hill. As the four came out of the forest another few soldier surrounded Shayra "Alright…if you want to die then who am I to stop you" said Shayra with a ball of flame in her hand.

Chapter-4

Shayra threw a fireball at the soldier and ran till the gate. Before the guard could attack, she dug her fingernails into the right side of his chest and slowed his breathing. As the other soldier came, she held him at the tip of her wand. She fired a spell at the other soldier knocking him out and tightening the fist punched the soldier on his heart so hard that he died on the spot. Soon a huge Minotaur ran at her but was held by her eyes which glowed and blasted him off. Shayra reached the door and with a flick of her wrist opened the gate "Come on Everyone the Door of Destiny waits for no one" shouted Shayra and entered the gate with Kiara, Tien, and Anubis entering behind her. As everyone entered the gates closed themselves and disappeared.

The Doors reappeared in a forest and everyone tumbled down like balls and fell on one another except for Shayra who flew out and stood in midair " Welcome to the Forest of Spirits the forest that houses every kind of magic creature fairies, mythical beasts, and other creatures" Shayra whistled and a Pegasus neighed at a distance and flew to her " Hello Kian nice to meet you" she said rubbing the snout of the Pegasus and summoned her magic staff which had a crystal ball held by talon-like projections from it " Let's go" she said patting the horse which took her into the air. They all went through the forest to a cottage.

Shayra opened the door and saw an old man limping and stooping around while mumbling something "Good Morning Grandpa, we require some information till the gates of the power core. Therefore, I want to go through my Gold book" said Shayra and went to him "Eh! You think I am doing what? Killing flies! Do it yourself. I cannot find the bottle of crushed dry moonflowers and marogs. Do you know where I kept it?" he asked in irritation "Here grandpa," she said waving her hand and making the bottle appear in it "Thank you, darling, there is a secret basement in the cottage which has a door that will lead you to the library of Alexandria. There you will find your Golden book, come with me" said the old man and escorted them till the library of Alexandria. He helped them by answering the question of Sphinx and found the book.

Shayra went through the book till she halted at a page "Guys look at this" she said pointing at a page on which it was written

The old man suddenly cried "I know where these gates of destiny are. Come with me" and he took them through a portal which made them land near a river. "Shayra my child! Take a dip in these waters while I recite the mystic verse" said the old man. Shayra entered The River of Purity and dipped herself within its depths while Solanis murmured the verses. Solanis at each spell threw the ashes of the passed away gatekeepers. He then took out a vial and said "Oh Goddess of Magic I summon you with the energy rested within me. Grant this noble one the power of magic and ancient power and remove the darkness if any" he said while pouring the contents of the vial into the river. Soon a glow appeared and the screech of an eagle, the river emitted a purple cloud.

A flash appeared and there standing in front of them was Shayra. Her eyes turned blue and the ears turned elven. She was dressed in a pure gold silk gown with a fan collar and elongated sleeve cuffs. Around her neck was a choker with an ancient ankh pendant, an oval ruby locket, and a crescent moon locket, her eyes changed to blue with a golden eyeshadow. Two huge wings sprouted from her back. Her nails were slightly long and were sharp enough to tear a heart as easily as plucking fruits and her fingers were decorated with rings of precious stones, around her head appeared a circlet made of gold with a central teardrop-shaped diamond and black hair formed a half ponytail at her back. " I am Shayra the Gatekeeper," she said giving a slight bow as everyone looked happily " It's time we have to go," said Solanis and they moved again to the Door of Destiny which this time took them to the mouth of a cave which was closed by a strange figure's body.

It was a woman whose hands and legs had ivy and vines twisted around them. Her skin was completely turned into tree bark except for her green eyes "Welcome Gatekeeper to the Cave of Powers and Prophecies, I am Ayana the Protector whom you elected" she said. Shayra quickly recognized her through the snake pendant around her neck "Who did this to you" she asked " Zakura he couldn't steal my heart, therefore, he used his dark magic and turned me into a half tree and left me as a seal to the gate" said Ayana and shed tears " Don't worry I will cure you" said Shayra and waved her hand over Ayana.

Soon, small blue wisps twisted themselves around Ayana. Soon, Ayana dematerialized into a cloud of golden smoke and rematerialized. Ayana was the most beautiful of all the celestial people with white skin and angled brows, her lips were rosy and nose was straight, her hair was brown which was tied into a high ponytail and she was wearing a fan collared full sleeve gown which was as green as her eyes. On her right wrist was a gold bangle bracelet and on her left-hand fingers were rings of emerald, jasper, gold. A leaf circlet rested on her forehead "Thank you for curing me Shayra" said Ayana and fell unconscious. Shayra quickly took Ayana in her lap and ran her hand over her body "The curse has taken a toll on her.

Grandpa takes her to the cottage" said Shayra, Solanis snapped his fingers and he and Ayana both disappeared in a blue cloud. Shayra took the three guardians to the inside of the cave. There in front of them were many obstacles and spirits that governed a golden chest "We have to be careful and quick to go till the chest" said Shayra and slowly demonstrated how to cross each obstacle. At end of all the obstacles, a fairy appeared and bowed to Shayra "I am Maya the fairy who guarded this place. I welcome you Gatekeeper and Guardians and allow you a safe passage" said the fairy and disappeared.

Shayra took the guardians to the final room where the chest was kept. Shayra went to the chest and placed the ankh pendant into the hole opening the chest. In the chest were three bracelets made of gold, silver, and copper respectively with three precious stones sapphire, ruby, and emerald in the center. A card with a precious metal border was placed in front of each bracelet. She took the silver bracelet with a sapphire in the center and a blue card with a silver border and gave them to Kiara. As she touched the card the bracelet flew at Kiara and attached itself to her wrist. Soon, Kiara glowed and turned into a warrior with silver armor and a sapphire circlet. In her hand appeared a short bow and, on her back, appeared a quiver full of arrows with swan feathers. On her finger appeared a scorpion ring with sapphires.

Shayra then took the gold bracelet with a ruby and a red card with a gold border who also morphed into a golden armor and helmet with a blazing sword at his back. Similarly, Tien got the copper bracelet with the emerald and was dressed in a copper armor and had a heavy hammer. The trio bowed in front of the gatekeeper who said "Arise my warriors. May the Mother Magic protect you and May Mother Nature defend you and May the Mother Spirit enable you to be able to do your work properly. May the Mother Wealth give you Prosperity and May Mother Knowledge help you with various kinds of knowledge. I am Proud of you the world is Proud of you. Be safe and be victorious" said Shayra and blessed them with her powers "Now let's go back," she said and waved her hands taking them back to the cottage.

As they entered the cottage, they saw Ayana lying on the bed and Solanis grinding herbs. Shayra ran to her side and taking her hand checked her pulse " Why hasn't she woken up yet" she asked " The Dark Magic broke but she is suffering from the poison that he placed on her body" " I know of a healing spell" said Kiara making everyone turn to her " What! When Leonor was training us, I did some reading on healing magic" said Kiara and took the ground medicine and using her magic dissolved it into the water and cast the spell on it.

She then gave the herb water to Ayana who was completely cured by it "Th…Th…Thank You" she said "It's all right Ayana" said Shayra and turned towards the Guardians "You got your power cores. Now go back and join the battle. I and the others will join you at the time of the Battle" she said. Kiara, Anubis, and Tien placed their hands on one another "Our purpose is done. We won. Now take us back to the original den" they said in a single voice and got teleported back into castle Amaris. "Good, you came back. A lot has happened since you left" said Athena escorting them to the hall.

As they entered the hall, they saw Arom, Lady Amarya, and Leonor with nine-ten other counselors who were reading the maps with a magnifying glass and checking inscriptions. Leonor ran and hugged the three and shaking their hands brought them back while narrating the purpose of the gathering "Zakura fooled us and took away the relics of ancient magic. He broke the neck of one soldier whereas crushed the heart of another. We fear he is using it for weapon" "We go to know but have you found any solution" asked Anubis

"Not yet prince we are searching," said Leonor, "I think if we consult a person with the knowledge of ancient powers maybe we can find a solution," said Iris "We know just the person," said Tien and whispered something into the ear of others. Soon they held each other's hands and shouted together "Shayra!" soon a cloud of golden smoke appeared and took shape and there was Shayra "

What happened" she asked "Shayra Zakura took a few relics of dark magic from the palace can you see what he is doing" asked Tien

"Sure Tien, I can," said Shayra and closed her eyes and suddenly opened them "Did he truly take what we fear," she asked Amarya "Yes, he did. That is why we are scared, what did you see?" she asked Shayra "He has placed them on an altar and using his powers is extracting their essence" answered Shayra "What did he steal" asked Anubis "Troll bones, ashes of the burned dark wizards and the strongest of them all the vial of black dust of Dark Magic" said Leonor " He is planning something very very bad. Something that will destroy us all and wipe out this realm once and for all" said Shayra and asked them all to gather around "We need to vacate this kingdom and go somewhere else to plan his destruction" said Shayra and placing the hand into her sleeve pulled out her wand and waved it in the air in a circular motion.

Amarya went to the balcony and stood facing the sky "Mother Let's go" said Arom "Son This castle was founded by me. I cannot let it be destroyed. You go keep Leonor safe and support him in his destiny" said Amarya and watched the fate as Leonor dragged Arom away and they both disappeared with others. Zakura stood in front of the altar and started extracting the essence of the relics. First, he placed his hand over the troll bones and as he twisted his hand up a purple-colored star appeared from it, similarly, he pulled out the essence of other things and merged them. Then he recited a verse and threw the orb on the Land of Wisdom and turned everyone to stone but could not affect Amarya. He appeared in the ruined fortress and took her as his prisoner with Amarya cursing "Soon, you eat your words and sleep in a grave. Soon you will get the greatest jolt of your life".

Shayra and the rest of the folk appeared in a cave and the others sat in the places they could find and Arom was saddened for leaving his mother behind while Leonor was consoling him "Leonor, Arom let's visit the ancient temple and seek the blessings of Goddess" said Shayra "You are right only the mother can help us in a hard time" said Leonor " We would like to see the temple" said Anubis " No! You must defend the cave and yourself. We will return shortly" said Shayra

She teleported herself, Leonor and Arom to the temple. The temple was a palace made completely out of nine metals and had different precious stones studded everywhere. The forest around the temple was inhabited by different kinds of fairies and serpents with knowledge of sorcery. Shayra went to the gate and placed her hand on it. Suddenly, there came a sound of opening lock and the gate opened. The trip went into the palace walked to the Shrine of the goddess.

As she reached the shrine the golden gates opened themselves revealing a black stone statue of the goddess sitting on a lion with two men sitting on either side of her on knees with folded hands. The goddess had ten hands and carried a chakra, a bow and arrow, a sword, a trident, a shield, a lotus, a mace, and a noose. Her hair was disheveled and she wore a crown. With her last two hands, she was blessing the devotees and telling them not to fear. On the left side of the goddess was a man with four hands.

In his first two hands, he carried a Phurba, and a Vajra and was folding his other two hands, the second man to the right was carrying a sickle and a vessel in his first two hands and was folding his last two hands. The goddess herself wore a garland of flowers on a red saree. Shayra bowed in front of the mother and kneeling recited her prayers. As she completed her prayers the statue of the goddess went up on a raised platform and revealed a chamber.

Shayra went into the chamber and moved to the basement. There in the basement were two candle stands with a book growing from a dried tree. Shayra opened the book and was surprised when a stanza in gold appeared in the book "Guys we found the Magic book which the goddess herself gifted to the Targula community. It was said that the book was lost but it was hidden by them here" said Shayra excitingly and started reading it. Soon, orange fumes appeared which Shayra inhaled into herself taking a deep breath with eyes closed. As she opened her eyes they shined with a blue light "We have to enhance the power of the guardians" she said and as she touched the book it turned into a short book which she placed in her bag.

She came out of the chamber and bowed in front of the mother and said with folded hands" Goddess you know the fate that is coming and has helped us now for it. Oh, mother goddess gives us your blessings like this forever" said Shayra and soon she heard a voice in her "Keep Safe the things you found" to which she replied out aloud "Sure Mother". They dematerialized from the temple into a golden cloud of smoke and reappeared in the cave.

Zakura was pacing near his throne restlessly thinking about a plan to search for the group of sorcerers for he got ma news from his spy that they disappeared just before the disintegration of the palace " I need them dead at any cost" he roared in the throne room " Maybe I can be of any help" came a voice. As Zakura turned in front of him was a tall skeletal figure clad in crow feathers wearing a black topaz ring with sharp nails on his fingers and toes "I am Corvan my lord a shadow warrior. I will pull those rats from their holes and give them to you" said the man in a voice that sounded like the cawing of a crow. Zakura gave him the permission he asked and sent him on the hunt. Using his magic tracker, he traveled to the cave for three days and four nights.

In the morning as the sun rose, he reached the tree that stood near the cave, and using his magic turned himself into a hover of crows. These hovers of crows flew out towards the cave and started cawing in the air. Shayra quickly recognized this as dark magic and cast a spell in the air saying "Darkus Conjures Destructum Corvus" Soon, all the crows started exploding, and those which were left returned and turned into Corvan who fired a black bolt and sent her back. Kiara quickly used her bracelet and using the water arrows fired them at Corvan who dodged them easily. Then Kiara placed her hand on her bottle and creating a whip tried to hit him but missed to which he laughed and giving a huge flutter he ascended into the sky and moved towards Kiara.

Chapter - 5

As Corvan was flying towards them a pure loud sound of a conch repelled him back. Kiara looked at the source of the sound and saw a youth standing with a conch in his hand. This youth was looking as if he was cursed for his left half was that of a tree and right half was that of a young elf man with a beardless smooth face and a tall well-built body where there were patches of tree bark. In his wrists, he wore wrist guards and a sword hung from his back. He wore a sleeveless brown tunic and elf boots with green trousers.

In his hand, he held a trident and stood in front of Corvan "Oh well if it isn't the young elf prince. You and your little troop are right on time for me to destroy" said Corvan sadistically. The young man aimed his trident at Corvan and casting a spell fired a bolt at him instantly burning his feathers "Nooooo! I am not through with you I will return" cried Corvan before dematerializing into a hover of crows but was soon caught by Leonor in a chest enchanted by him "Thank you" said Leonor to Ciaran. The young man turned but suddenly Kiara hugged him and kissed him.

Soon, the young man started to change and all the bark on him turned to dust making him a complete man. As he was shocked by the turn of events Magic appeared in front of them "Kiara your heart responded to his heart and you got your true love which made him well" said Magic " thank you, Kiara, you have broken my curse" said the young man " What is your name sir?" asked Tien " I am Ciaran the Lord of the Northern mountain tribe. This place is not safe for you to come with me" said Ciaran and took them deep into the forest.

After a long-distance he whistled and a stout black ram cane running "Welcome to my kingdom Lords and Ladies" said Ciaran and asked them to sit on the mounts which were a herd of black ram " I found them when they were just children and took care of them" He told Kiara who listened attentively to him. Soon they crossed the tunnel and there was the Northern tribe. This tribe consisted of Centaurs and lion cubs who lost their pride. Soon an old woman came to Ciaran and kissed him on his forehead "The leader is back" she shouted "Ma these people are hiding from their enemy and have been attacked"

"We are always warm to the refugees please come," she said sending them to their place "And this girl is Kiara. She broke my curse" as Ciaran mentioned it a huge whisper erupted among the people "What happened?" Ciaran asked the old woman "Son, today is the valuable day Hayamara or the day of union. The breaking of your curse today shows that you are made for each other" She said happily "What is Hayamara" asked Moris "It is the day when the two lovers Hayati and Amaron sacrificed themselves to create a peaceful kingdom.

The gods blessed them and turned their souls into stars with a blessing that after every twenty-five years these stars will merge as one. The body they left turned into two huge serpents who were tasked with protecting us from evil spirits. So, our ancestors introduced Hayamara and we celebrate it every twenty-five years said the old woman "Guys let me introduce you to my secret battalion of soldiers" said Ciaran and took them to a place.

There they saw people with strong muscles and strength and agility far greater than a human being "These are my army. They are not werewolves but are stronger than them. They are not vampires but are swifter than them. I call the Beasts" As he called upon the name the people turned towards him and snarled like feline beasts. Their skins were tanned and eyes were like those of cats. The men's hair was either short cropped or crew cut and women's hair was in a half-braided style "Let me demonstrate their skills" said Ciaran and whistled.

One of the Beasts climbed a tree and watched here and there. As he sensed a danger he jumped directly on the man and broke his neck "Marvelous work Lord Ciaran" said Arom "thank you Lord Arom. I would like to contribute them to your secret army" said Ciaran "Agreed It would be great to have such mercenary warriors on our side" said Arom. At night, the tribes celebrated the Hayamara festival with great pomp and show. The great Goddess was worshipped and feasts were arranged.

Everyone enjoyed the festival to the end. After the end of the celebrations, everyone returned to their places. Anubis was lost in dreams "Permission to enter" came a voice. Anubis turned to see and was dumbfounded when Cynthia was standing in front "Seems like you are lost in some thought. I will come back later" said Cynthia "No not at all," said Anubis and started talking with her.

Zakura was waiting impatiently for Corvan when a spy returned "What happened?" he asked "Corvan is dead my Lord. They have gathered new allies and armies to fight you my Lord" said the spy. Zakura immediately killed the soldier telekinetically with a flick of the wrist by breaking his neck. Zakura's screams filled the air. As Amarya heard the screams she understood that they were Zakura's the corner of her withered lips smiled.

Zakura quickly ran into the prison and shouted "Where are they" "Zakura heed my advice and leave now or else you shall not return forever. You inflicted more damage on me than protecting your kingdom. If you will not leave the whole kingdom shall suffer. Your death is arriving stop it if you can" she said. That night Zakura could not sleep. His nightmares were strong to be affected by dreamcatchers or poppets. In his dream, he saw the battlefield flowing with blood. Fires were destroying every house. He saw himself on the ground unable to move.

Leonor walked in front of him with the head of a soldier in one hand and a sword bathed in blood. He was begging for his life but Leonor was not listening. Then he saw death as a hooded figure carrying away the souls to hell and killing the rest with his scythe. On one hand, he held his scythe while with the other he held a clock "Your time is up" said he in a monotonous voice pointing his finger at the Zakura who was trembling with fear. This made him suddenly jump from his sleep and scream.

"Lady Aquila I would like to test your worth to a powerful weapon I created," said Moris twisting and waving his hand. Soon, a chest made of gold and wood appeared. Moris snapped his hand and the chest opened to reveal a Chakra made of iron was placed in the middle of the box. "This is a weapon I forged using the various spells and scriptures. I want you to lift it" he said. Aquila placed her hand on the chakra and lifted it as if it was made of wood. As she held the chakra in her hand it began to burn but it did not harm her "You are worthy, accept it as a gift from me" said Moris and directed her to use it. Aquila with her strength threw the chakra towards the forest with cutting the trees as easily as if snapping twigs. As it returned, she harmlessly grabbed it and placed it on her waist and thanked Moris "It's my pleasure princess. I forged it for the worthy" said Moris as Kiara, Anubis and Tien entered "Ah you are right on time" He said running hither thither around the camp and finally grabbing a jewel box

"I thought of teaching you a few binding spells which of course Leonor would have taught you," he said by placing the jewel box on the table. As he opened the box there was in it a garland of shining oyster pearls "A pearl set. What do you expect us to attract him" asked Kiara "Be careful when you speak Water Guardian? These are not normal pearls. These are enchanted pearls which I am going to activate using a series of magic powers. So, if you are thinking like a peasant girl then I believe you have no business in war councils said Moris angrily

"You should never doubt Moris. He is one of the powerful wizards in my council" said a voice and as everyone turned around they found Leonor standing at their back in a White full sleeve tunic and white trousers wearing a white pearl ring "What have you made this time he asked joining Moris " I am about to make a string of pearls enough to bind an evil entity and drain him of his powers, but for that, I would require a spell enchantment from you with constant firing of energy balls made of spells to prevent him from moving as these pearls will immobilize and after I combine the power of light and white magic it will because burns if he tries to escape" said Moris "What a fantastic plan. Sorry for doubting you Lord Moris" said Kiara "No problem Dear, I understand your misconception seeing the pearl garland, and therefore I would require the help of you three as well. Please cross your wrists with the amulets" said Moris and they did as instruct creating a triangle.

Moris enchanted a spell and drained the tiniest bit of their power enough to create a small orb. Moris waved his hand drawing a triangle with a circle on each of the three points on the ground. He placed the orb in the first circle. Then he used the rays of the sun creating a new orb and placed it into the second circle. At last, he placed his hand in the taking position, and summoning all his energy created a small orb of light and threw it into the third circle thereby filling the three corners of the triangle. He then brought the garland and placed it in the center and stepped back. Then he started chanting "Lightiumn Grantius Energia" thereby energizing the pearls strongly. Soon all the energies merged into the neckpiece which started shining.

Moris brought the neckpiece and called Shayra. He gave her the necklace and said "It requires a little bit of your magic and then Kiara will carry it" said Moris "But why Kiara" asked Shayra "Kiara may not be a leader but knows her responsibility quite well than any other. She is gonna be tasked after the war to escort the Beasts, Wind Keepers, and Wizard-Witch Knight soldiers to the faraway lands with Ciaran, Aronil, Valarus, and the tribes so that the changes they did should not be going into wrong hands and the discoveries should remain hidden. Therefore, she would require the talents of not only a Guardian but also those of a Protector so she would require this necklace and can only use it five times.

Therefore, please energize it" said Moris. Shayra gave her powers to the pearls and gave it to Kiara without mentioning the future to her.

Zakura went through the book of Darkness and found a spell which he cast on the graves thereby awakening the souls of dead warriors and built his army. He gathered his warriors for the attack. As Moris was roaming out of the tent he saw a hooded figure "Who are you" asked Moris "My name in Omenor. I am a wizard who works for the Magna Eye the society that keeps the order. I want to battle on your side and have been sent here by the temple of Ardoria" said Omenor removing his hood and revealing his handsome face with lightly tanned skin, black eyes and short-cropped black hair swept towards his right. His nose was straight and his ears were simple like normal humans. His cloak was black and ragged and he wore a ruby ring and his boots were pointed as well. Soon, they were interrupted by a purring and as they turned, they saw the Mau sitting there "Its lady Amarya's cat. If it is here then it means it has brought a message"

"Amarya wanted us to know that She was abducted. But thank God we got the message before that by torturing Corvan. I believe Zakura might be thinking Corvan is dead" said Iris with everyone sighing in relief. Shayra took the cat into her tent to take care of it. Leonor came to Omenor and welcomed him warmly and graciously to his team and council to which Omenor bowed to him and promised his allegiance to Leonor to which Leonor said "I am honored to have a great warrior like you on our side. If ever you wish to leave you will not pressurized that's my promise" said Leonor giving him his vow to which Omenor agreed and joined the group and as if his presence invited allies a sorceress appeared in front "I am Zoara the witch of Norbag I wish to join the council as well with my brother Dormir" she said pointing at the man standing on her side. Zoara and her brother were twins in every aspect of appearance with black hair, white skin, and pointed nose. But Zoara wore a brown gown and her brother an overcoat trimmed with fur. Zoara wore a circlet with a pair of feathers hanging on either side of her temple. She wore an amethyst ring. Her brother Dormir had a crew cut hair with a neatly trimmed beard and a band of silver on his finger "Welcome with your arrival we are complete" said Leonor and with all the official work joined them as well.

The next morning Leonor invited everyone to his camp "I called you all here to discuss the details of the battle plan. Therefore, I recommend you to have your seats" he said pointing at the seats. As everyone sat he started explaining to the plan " Guys as we all know that an I with the permission of my brother His Majesty Lord Arom and the Elder Queen Lady Amarya built a secret army of ninety-five thousand troops of which fifty percent are flying witch army and the rest are on foot wizard army armed with swords, spears, wands, and spells.

"Recently, Lord Ciaran and Lord Aronil have provided us with five thousand troops of the Beast army and five thousand troops of Wind Keepers. The Guardian Anubis has called from his City an army of Fifteen thousand-foot soldiers and Lord Walvarus has provided us with five thousand troops of water soldiers and five thousand ships with soldiers and armory. So according to my Arithmetic calculation, we have one lakh thirty thousand troops of soldiers under our banner with three judiciaries three generals three guardians"

"three leaders a gatekeeper the four Masters and three of members of my wizard council. Therefore, all of you will be divided into five groups with four generals getting a one lakh twenty-five thousand five hundred troops of soldiers each. While Tengula and Aquila will sneak in with Omenor, Zoara, and Dormir to get the refugees and the Queen back. Therefore, this will be an attack both from the outside and inside. With that we can conquer and destroy Zakura finally."

said Leonor and occasionally tapped the chart hanging at his

back with a cane he held in his hand "

Chapter -6

In the morning, Ciaran and Aronil stood out of the tent and said in a unified voice "We summon The Goddess of War to get us success and the Lord to protect us" and then drawing a deep breath blew a conch so loudly that the eight directions trembled with the sound. Then the five groups went forward with Leonor carrying the Refugee Rescue Group with him. After three days of traveling, they reached till the realm of fairies and camped there.

In the night while they were reviewing the battlefield strategies Moris sensed something and went out with an energy orb in his hand and would have thrown it when the person came out in the open "Wait for Lord Moris I am here on behalf of the fairy queen a brought you this" she said giving him a small round narrow neck bottle full of pink dusty substance " Is it fairy dust?" he asked "Yes collected from the purest aura of fairies and mixed with the rays of the sun" said the fairy "Tell your queen that I thanked her for her help" said Moris and the fairy flew away.

Moris burst into his tent and waving his hand he created a cauldron and after pouring water snapped his fingers lighting the fire and started stirring " First a few purest pearls from the depth of the seas" he said throwing a few pearls into the water "Then the blood of the purest soul" he said pouring a drop of blood "Next to the moondust" he said blowing a fistful of white dust into the water "Then a while of Phoenix essence, ashes left after the death of Phoenix mixed its tears" he said pouring a bottle of black liquid and stirred it " Now a small pinch of fairy dust" he said adding the fairy dust. As the fairy dust mixed the dark red substance it became colorless.

He then took three vials and poured a small quantity of the potion and placing them in their holder he casted a spell on them "potions in the vial be strong use your power to bind the wrong" as he casted a spell the vials gave a shine and then became normal. He invited the Guardians into his tent and gave them the vials and said "I made this for the binding spell. It will strengthen the bond of the pearls. You have to throw the vials as soon as the pearls surround Zakura" he said handing over the vials to the three Guardians and they thanked him and went away.

Omenor waved his hand and summoned a mirror "Show me her" he said and soon a reflection appeared of a woman " So what happened" asked the woman " I joined the council and have given them the exact correct directions and told them the truth that I work for Magna Eye" said Omenor "Excellent, Magna Eye is proud of you. Your motive is to aid the Guardians and to stay with Kiara and Ciaran for their future aid and hide the alliance between us and Moris from everyone" said the lady. Omenor waved his hand and made her image disappear when Moris entered "I am happy for you to be here. Kiara and Ciaran would require the aid of maximum people including Zoara and Dormir" he said "I promise my Lord I won't disappoint you" said Omenor.

Moris went into Leonor's tent " The prophecy will be fulfilled soon but what about the aftermath, is it inevitable for Kiara and Anubis to leave the Guardians to escort the Beasts with the three allies" he asked " Yes, for the sake of the safety of the world she needs to go with the allies" said Leonor and clapped his hands, a servant brought a tray with six small boxes " These are the powers we are going to give the allies" said Leonor and opened the boxes revealing six precious rings, pointing at the silver dragon ring he said " This one is for Omenor" then he pointed at the golden phoenix ring " that's for Zoara" at last pointing at the other three silver rings with a raven, a wolf, and an emerald cobra he said " They will be for the rest three" and he at last picked a copper ring with a red topaz " that is for the last guardian who will go with Kiara" he said with an air of mystery which Moris didn't like " Don't keep it a secret let it be out" said Moris impatiently " I will but after the final battle, till then bear some patience old friend" said Leonor and gave him a warm and understanding hug which ultimately won Moris over and he went off.

Cynthia was sitting near the river when Kiara and Shayra came to her " Seems someone is in deep thoughts" said Shayra " Oh nothing it's just…" said Cynthia " I know you are thinking about Anubis aren't you" asked Kiara "Yes I think I am in love with him but I and he are the Masters of two different elements how can we be together" asked Cynthia to which Kiara waved her hand and brought from the river a bubble and gave it to Cynthia who turned it into a ball of ice " Look at yourself Cynthia you can control ice and so does he despite he can only do so until the bracelet is with him but with your emergence, this will a wonder where Ice and Fire can live with one another without harming anyone of the two. Therefore, forget your worries and tell him what you think" said Kiara and they left her to ponder.

Anubis was also facing the same problem and therefore he talked about it with Tien and Moris who also convinced him to leave the doubt and talk to Cynthia but before he could a letter came from Cynthia

Anubis

I want to talk to you wholeheartedly and convey something to you

Cynthia

Anubis was confused therefore he decided to go and meet Cynthia. In the moonlight, by the beach shore, he saw Cynthia sparkling like a star with her white clothes and silver jewelry. He asked Cynthia "Why did you call me?" "I wanted to say that I am in love with you," said Cynthia which made Anubis jump to cloud nine and smile happily and confess that he loves her too. Kiara, Shayra, Moris, Tien, and Ciaran hid behind the boulders and heard them confess but soon heard the walking sound of someone and peeped to see the servant going to disturb them. Tien flicked his wrist and pulled the servant behind the boulder with the help of an ivy " Let them savor their love you blithering idiotic good for nothing old bat!" said Tien and kept him there till Anubis and Cynthia enjoyed their moment by Cynthia laying with her head resting in Anubis's shoulder and placing her hand on his hand. It seemed that love was in the air for Leonor confessed his love to Shayra who agreed to it with her heart. Moris and Shayra kissed each other and confessed their love to each other.

 Moris called Aquila to his lair and after a little stir gave her the powder in a pouch "it is a sleeping powder of a pinch of used tea leaves and a large amount of dried and crushed poppy flowers. One whiff and you will sleep for four hours. Be careful to blow it on the face of your enemy" said Moris and gave the pouch to her. After giving Aquila the pouch of sleep powder Moris instructed her on how to enter the castle in the night and sent his sister Floressa with her. As per his instructions, Aquila disguised herself as a peasant woman with a magic spindle who had the ability to leave beautiful garments. The others refugee rescuers were instructed to be her assistants whereas Floressa was told to praise the peasant in front of the soldiers and then they all were to take the dust that Moris made and blow it into people's eyes and send them to sleep.

As per the plan, the spindle was placed on a cart and Aquila sat on it weaving the cloth while two stout bulls pulled the cart to the kingdom the rest of the five people walked at Aquila's back hailing her as "Kaya the witch Tailor". As she neared the gate the soldiers stopped her and asked who she was when Floressa told them about her immense powers and even said that the one who touches the needle of her spinning wheel shall instantly become invincible. These tales were so convincing that the soldiers went to the king and begged him to touch the spindle needle.

Meanwhile, Aquila enchanted the needle with a sleeping spell and asked the others to knock the soldiers and clear the area. Soon, each took a fistful of dust and knocked out the soldiers and hid them away. As Zakura came out he couldn't resist touching the spinning wheel and needle but suspects the pheasant which she sensed and said: " Sire I know thou doubts me, I thou doesn't want to win the battle then I will be on my way" at which the king willingly rotated the wheel but unknowingly pricked his finger knocking himself out for a complete fortnight.

This was enough for the Refugee group who entered the castle by covering their mouths with a silk cloth and blowing the powder on the way. Soon they reached the prison and killed the guards. Then they one by one released all the prisoners, humiliated and tortured people. In the end, they reached the prison where Amarya was held, and breaking the spells that hold her they took her away. Omenor with his magic knowledge healed the prisoners of the wounds and scars and disguised them as villagers. Aquila again took her place on the spindle and in the same way returned to the camp without even the slightest knowledge to the kingdom and the guards. Everyone at the camp was happy with the refugee group and praised them for what they did.

Every one of the prisoners was tended to and were cured of the horrors of the prison. Leonor at night took a torch and went for a walk. There in the middle of the resting refugees was a twenty-year-old young man who had a full beard and long hair and could not speak. Leonor sat with him and held his neck "in the name of the powerful magic I command the voice of this boy to return" he whispered and asked the boy to open his mouth. Soon, green fumes came out of the boy's mouth and mixed into the air "Now try to speak" said Leonor "He…Hel…Help!" he said and started hugged Leonor

"Thank you," said The boy "What is your name?" asked Leonor " I am Thoren, I was captured by Zakura and tortured by him, he made me his servant and do his menial jobs, I was constantly tortured and tormented, he kept me cuffed by the neck like an animal and treated me in the ways he liked, I was publicly shamed by him and had stones thrown at me by the people. Today, you and your kind freed me from his clutches. I wish you would win the battle and destroy him" said Thoren teary-eyed and hugged Leonor with respect and thanked him.

But his story left a mark on Leonor who now hated Zakura even more.

Amarya sat on a chair before the battle plans and thought for some time she then clapped her hands. A soldier came running "I want to participate in this battle, go to Iris and tell her to bring the chest" said Amarya. The soldier ran out and met Iris giving her the message. Iris ran to Amarya with a heavy wooden chest and gave it to her. As she opened it, she saw there in the box a white gown, a silver masquerade mask with a curved beak, and a folded tessen fan with a small box. Amarya opened the box and saw a bracelet with a tiger eye "This bracelet was gifted to me by my love whom I lost because of Zakura" said Amarya shedding tears and kissing the bracelet. As she wore the bracelet it changed her.

Her normal human form changed into a deadly warrior. Her finger and toenails became sharp. On her eyes appeared the silver masquerade mask with a curved beak. From her back sprouted to eagle wings. She held the tessen fan in her right hand and covered her face partially with it while giggling like a girl " You look fierce my lady" said Iris " Thanks to Iris" said Amarya and touched the bracelet turning into a human " Will your son be happy knowing that you hid a secret for the welfare of the kingdom" asked Iris "This battle needs to be fought with everything we have therefore my sons will require a greater help in the fight. Remember, you shall not reveal this secret to either of them" said Amarya "I swear on my life Amarya. Your sons will not hear of this secret from me" said Iris and hugged Amarya " May this war remove all the past problems" she said " Don't worry, the end of battle night shall awaken a day of hope for us all" said Amarya patting Iris on her back and sending her with a good night. In the morning, after the sound of trumpets, conches, and blessings the army was ready to attack and walked towards the palace of Zakura.

Zakura woke from his sleep bewildered and angry and the first thing he did was to command the ones who told him about the spindle to be beheaded. The greater shock came to him when he heard from his spies that the army of Leonor was five days away from the castle and three days away from the border. His frenzy made the whole castle tremble with fear. He commanded his leftover army to get ready within five days for battle. The poor souls of the human soldiers were already trembling with the imaginative results of the war and the command of Zakura sent the poor things helter-skelter like hens and cocks giving up hope on their lives. No one could tell Zakura what was the situation of his army with the current circumstances.

After two days the Great Army of Amaris and other kingdoms reached the river crossing to the border of Netheria. At the night Leonor heard a few whispers from the outside and went to check there standing in front of him we are his ancestral mothers the Nymphs appeared. He talked to them wholeheartedly and spent his night with them who repeated the story of his birth and recounted how small he was and how they gave him up to the kingdom of Amaris for his protection.

Every one of the men made a campfire and toasted for the upcoming battle with Leonor again repeating their plan with secret dampening spells and spy detection spells as a defense. After that, they all slept for a whole night as if there is no tomorrow and the next day trained half the day and began the journey again till the next day when they reached the border of the kingdom. They rested in the village on the border for one day and reached the kingdom before night for the next day battle.

Chapter-7

They reached the fort and announced the war. Zakura armored himself and decided to once talk to his army. He tried best ways to pump the army with energy but every bit of his word failed to breach the thick skulls of the poor miserable army who feared the creatures that are gonna be unleashed. In the end, they decided to become the heifers but with a tough fight like a true army because they knew that they are going to be the feast for the Beasts and Wind keepers and knew that the army of Amaris greatly outnumbered them.

The armies faced each other as the afternoon approached. Zakura after a face-off with Leonor through words summoned the army of the dead but was blinded to the painful fact that the generals of the army included witches and wizards. The mortal soldiers were just happy to outnumber their foes but were given a tight slap on their cheeks by the bad luck as they realized the fact the commanders were also experts in magic and cursed the king like anything. Moris signaled to Athena to send back the dead and let the war begin. Athena left her steed and stepping into the open cast a spell saying

Hells scream heavens chime,

End the undead soldiers' time

The tail of Dragon Phoenix's eye

Let these souls in the fires of hell

Be fry. With spells that I read

Send this evil back to the realm of dead

Her spell caused the earth to crack and sent all the zombies back to the place from where they came and filled the earth with their screams as they were pulled back into hell " That's not fair, you are breaking the rules of battle" said Zakura "Says the person who betrayed his kingdom for the sake of a darker power. These words from your filthy mouth are the same as that of the culprit when he refuses his crimes" rebuked Leonor "You are a coward. Army forward" screamed Zakura "It is you who summoned your impending doom. Charge!" shouted Leonor, Ciaran commanded the Beasts to tear the soldiers apart. The Beasts as they ran seemed like merciless lions who were about to pounce on the bleating herd of sheep. The Wind keepers took to the skies and lifting each soldier by shoulders flung them so hard on the ground that their bones turned to dust. The Beasts started fighting the ground soldiers who tried to wound them but merely scratched their skins.

The Beasts in even a greater furry held the soldiers by their hands and tore them into two. Some of the soldiers tried to beg for mercy but they killed them by tearing off their heads. The mortal army of Amaris also fought the battle but the army of Zakura could not fight for the fear of which Beast will tear them apart and which Wind Keeper would throw them on the groundbreaking their bones.

Zakura commanded Deviles his commander to attack with Corruptusbut they both could not stand against Leonor. Arom also slashed Zakura's army with his sword. The Witch Council destroyed the Dark witches and wizards one by one. Soon Amarya saw a person about to attack Arom from the back and taking her beast form jumped into battle slashing and blowing the soldiers with her tessen fan. Kiara created a water ring that sharp as a sword and killed the soldiers. Anubis fired fireballs at the soldiers. Only a handful of soldiers were left after the mayhem.

They ran to Leonor and begged him "Sire we are at your mercy, save us from this chaos and mayhem of death. Standing in the middle of the battle we see death dancing with skulls for garland and a billhook in hand. Your Beasts tore our colleagues from their very limbs. Your Wind Keepers threw us from skies breaking our bones. The water girl cut us to pieces. The fire boy roasted us like vegetables. The earth boy crushed us under his rocks. They ignored our bleats. Please have mercy. Zakura lost his humanity but we swear we won't" said the soldiers, Leonor turned and saw Shayra fighting a voodoo wizard and destroying him with a single bolt. He saw Zoara and Dormir destroying the army.

Heaven saw a Beast dragging a soldier by his limb and tearing him to pieces. He saw the Beast form of his mother destroy the enemies. He looked at Moris "Kill the rest, let these ten soldiers live" he said and turned away " You are merciful, from now on we serve you" said the soldiers and took up arms from dead soldiers of Amaris and killed their kind " Traitors, how dare you disobey your King. I shall kill you" shouted Zakura and as he rose his hand to cast a curse, quickly Moris signaled Kiara who pulled her garland of pearls and threw them towards Zakura.

The pearls created a circle around Zakura and trapped him in the ring. Slowly, his powers started draining from his body and entering the pearls. Zakura could not repel the magic and fell to his knees "Zakura always remembers no matter how strong evil is it falls to its knees in front of good" said Leonor while Moris chanted "Darower Darkum Drainius" and asked the three Guardians to throw in the vials. The Guardians threw the vial into the ring making it more powerful. Every time Zakura tried to raise to his feet he was electrocuted and fell back to his knees due to the enchantment of the pearls. Leonor, after the process was over, waved his hand and made the pearls back to a garland and gave it back to Kiara.

Everyone walked to their mounts leaving Zakura on his knees on the battlefield. "I cannot be defeated so easily; they have taken my power but they cannot defeat me. If I will die, I will also end the reason for my death" thought Zakura and lifted the bow on his side and placing the arrow aimed at Leonor. "Leonor!" shouted Zakura making Leonor stop with his back to Zakura and place his hand on the hilt of his dagger "If I am going down, I will take you with me," said Zakura and released the arrow. Leonor closed his eyes to let death take him but it seemed death was interested in someone else for Leonor heard the scream of his brother and turned to find him on the ground with the arrow in his chest "Arom!" shouted everyone and collected around him While Leonor stood bewildered at the events when suddenly everything became clear to him.

He fell to his knees and taking his brother's head in his lap wailed loudly and stared at Zakura with red eyes "You shouldn't have done that Zakura" said Leonor teary-eyed "You took away my brother, the person I loved and respected.

You took away the hope of Amaris. I will not let you live" screamed Leonor and taking his sword ran at him when Moris quickly hugged him and whispered in his ear "Let the anger go! He doesn't deserve it" and turned Leonor away from Zakura who laughed madly and mocked him. Leonor could not bear the laughter of evil lord and in a reflex threw his dagger which lodged itself squarely in Zakura's chest while blood came from his mouth. Aquila also pulled out her quoit and beheaded Zakura by throwing the razor-sharp chakra at him.

The whole kingdom and the warriors mourned Arom and with a heavy heart did his funeral by burying him and placing a golden triangle on his chest with three olive leavers in the center and hiding it with mud. Leonor then stepped forward and using his powers created an orb of light "The Kingdom of Amaris mourns the loss of its King. The noble and most valiant knight and a kind, generous king. When he rode the battlefield on his black stallion with his curved sword, even the soldiers of evil begged for mercy. We shall never forget you Arom" said Leonor and placed the light orb on the grave

A year after the battle

"We fought a war for the sake of every living soul. We lost many lives and gained many allies. We met various people who were troubled by a ruthless evil king and brought them under one roof. One whom we called ours betrayed us but we united our force and destroyed him. Maybe King Arom has left us but on the persuasion and request of the great queen Amarya her adopted son Lord Leonor shall be our ruler and the supreme of the Tribunal" said Osiris. Soon the throne room gates opened and Leonor walked towards the throne and ascended the steps.

As he took his place on the throne Amarya placed the bejeweled crown on his head and declared him King "Let the celebrations begin" said Osiris with an uproar of applause from the people. Each king from a province provided a gift of money, arms, cloths, magic artifacts, and some ancient ruins which Leonor took and thanked them with promises. Then, he gestured to his soldier and whispered in his ear "Tell the Guardians, Witch Council, Judiciary, Generals and the Royal Mother to meet me in my private chamber". The soldier ran around the hall whispering from ear to ear and telling them that it is king order.

"Why have you called us here," asked Anubis as everyone met in the private chamber "There is an urgent matter to discuss. More important than my coronation" said Leonor "What is it son?" asked Amarya "Mother as you know in the war, we were helped not only by our mortal army but also by the exceptional Beasts and Wind Keepers. But before this battle could begin I heard a prophecy which said that these great powers would have to be hidden away with their respective scrolls or else this will destroy the earth by falling into the wrong hands" said Leonor which made the whole group discuss among themselves " Then they should be hidden away, but who will do that" asked Zorek "I have the solution for that as well but it is hard and emotionally painful" said Leonor " What is it?" asked Tien

"Two of the three Guardians have been chosen by the prophecy who are assigned this task of Keepers," said Leonor "Who are they?" asked Aquila "Anubis and Kiara," said Leonor which turned the whole group speechless. Soon, Anubis and Kiara stepped forward after a small discussion "I and Kiara are ready to take up the job without any conditions" said Anubis surprising the group even more " Then you both shall leave tomorrow after your marriage with all the facilities to two different kingdoms, Kiara and Ciaran will go to the northern realm whereas Anubis and Cynthia shall go to the southern realm" said Leonor " Sure, but who will we be accompanied with?" asked Anubis " Kiara will be accompanied by Athena, Omenor and Nefertiti and Anubis will be accompanied by Zoara Dormir and Tygart. These six people will be given six rings as a mark of their council tomorrow" said Leonor and dismissed the council.

The next morning a great ceremony was held where all the members including the king himself had their marriages conducted with the couple's sipping the elixir from an ancient cup while all the witches hissed to ward off evil spirits and wizards read the Spell of Bonding. After that Leonor's wife, Shayra was crowned the queen and he gave away the rings to all the six members. Nefertiti got the golden phoenix ring, Tygart got the tiger ring, Athena got the silver snake ring, Omenor got the dragon ring, Zoara got the raven shape ring, and in the end, Dormir got the wolf ring. After ceremoniously gifting away the rings, Leonor explained the matter to the whole court and sent Kiara and Anubis to their respective kingdoms respectfully.

After entering their Kingdom Kiara assigned Athena with the hiding process, Athena took Nefriti and Omenor and went through the hallway till they reached a chamber. Athena opened the chamber which was wide enough to house three lakh quartets of the army. She waved her hand and summoned pedestals made of stone. Then she asked each Beast to stand on a pedestal. As the whole Beast army stood on their respective pedestals Athena opened her spell book and placed a charm on the soldiers turning them to stone for eternity

" Only a person with my blood can open this gate," said Athena and went to Omenor " My love, remember only our child can open this gate," said Athena to which Omenor hugged her " For twelve years, after you left the Spell College I thought I lost my love, but now I am happy for us," said Omenor and hugged her and confessed his love for her. Nefertiti was in the thoughts of Dormir when Omenor woke her up sharing his happiness.

A woman walked into the battlefield. She was looking like a sunken skeleton with a black figure, hair wearing a hood and an iron nail "brother your death shall not go in vain, I shall take your revenge. This is the promise of Adrazelle" said the woman scratching the skeleton with her nail. She screamed aloud terrifying the eight directions. Then she hugged the skeleton for one last time before telling her soldiers to carry it away for its funeral. As she followed the carriage, she saw the apparition of her master an old man wearing dirty rags and carrying a crooked stick "to exact your revenge you must first steal the book it can only help with the first phase of your revenge" said the master. Thanking him she promised everlasting destruction and followed her brother for his last rites which she performed with the feeling of grudge, sorrow, anger, and hatred

Epilogue

Kiara gave a glance at the Beasts who Athena turned into statues and asked Omenor " Seal the gate and keep an eye on it, from now on you will be the Keeper of the Beasts" said Kiara and giving him a hug she walked out of the cave and met Ciaran " Is the battle over?" she asked doubtfully " yes it was over " said Ciaran " Then why am I feeling that this battle is far from over?" asked Kiara to which Ciaran gave her a warm kiss of relief and comfort to her paining soul

Anubis and Cynthia after the kiss released each other's grip on each other and saw from a distance the cave in which they hid the secret Wind keepers as statues and gave away the work to Zoara and Dormir " I don't think the battle was over because I think someone will surely return to fight us" said Anubis " Then we will send them back from whence they came" said Cynthia and rested her head on Anubis's shoulder while looking at the moon." Shayra we need to be careful, we hid the secrets with the Guardians but soon a new trouble is going to arise" said Leonor " Well as the power to guard we will surely defeat any about to arise problems and also we have the power to call the Guardians, therefore don't worry and let the Supreme Power handle everything" said Shayra and hugged Leonor" I don't fear the trouble I already lost Arom. I cannot tend to lose any of my other loved ones and that includes you"

" Tien you need to concentrate and fight for you have to be equally powerful like the Anubis Kiara" said Amarya while remembering the loses and horrors of the war and teaching Tien a few more skills to fight while Medusa Zorek Tengula and the judiciary looked upon them looked upon them " I think she is still not able to get over from her son's death and the horrors she faced" said Zorek " the queen will overcome them as she is the strongest person we ever met and worked with" said Medusa and taking Zorek moved within the castle.

Nefriti came to Omenor "I think I shall stay with you for a while and keep an eye at the gate" she said "No problem" stammered Omenor. "If you don't mind can I stay with you" asked Tygart to which Zoara nodded while Dormir happily shied away averting his eyes from the couple and looked at the flying birds and smiling. A man was travelling through kingdoms till he reached a graveyard. He walked in there and searched for the grave of his mistress. There he found three statues each of a lady with four hands and deshelled hair adorned with a flower circlet. The rock gowns were adorned with vines and moss. The first statue carried a pitcher, few herbs, sword, and shield. The second statue carried a spear, a book, a noose while blessing with the fourth hand. The third and last statue carried a serpent, a quoit, and aimed an arrow with the third and fourth hand.

"In the presence of the great ancestral witches, I conduct the ritual, Arya, Aranya, Aleera hear my plea to bring forth a noble soul, the battle begins the good needs help. Gather your powers and summon Minarya back" said the man. Suddenly, the three statues emitted a strong yet powerful ray of light merging it into one united force which opened the ground of the graveyard and summoned a comet of smoke. This comet flew out and after a few twists and turns dashed itself against the center exploding into a mound of ash. The man walked towards the mound and stood their shedding tears "My queen its time you come back to life to win over the treacherous evil" he said and pulled out a small coin with some ancient language and placed it in the middle of the mound.

Then he pulled out a vial of liquid "the water from the seven holy rivers may flow like blood in her" he said while pouring the liquid on the coin. Then he pulled out eight candles "I burn these eight candles already burned in eight houses which heard good and auspicious news to the eight guardians for my mistress' resurrection" and burned a candle in each direction while reciting a spell of ancient language in a sing song way. As he burned the final candle he stepped back. Suddenly, the eight candles became eight points which formed an eight pointed octa gram " I balanced the dark with the light, I summoned the witches presence, I call upon thee oh supreme power to resurrect the queen who was once a sister and a queen to return back for the forth coming battle" said the man and threw fistful of dust into the light made octa gram which started to spin in the ninth and central void and finally created a huge twister merging with ashes of his late queen while creating occasional lightening.

Suddenly, he heard a cackle of witches and saw that the three witches have appeared at the three points of the octa gram giggling and cackling with laughter "Art thou surprised to see us lad" asked Arya " He is sis can't thou see his surprised look" asked Aranya " We are here to aid thee with our powers to resurrect thy noble queen, thou called us to bless but we are here to aid thee" said Aleera. The three witches lifted their hands in the sky and cried "Oh Gods here our plea. We the old summon thee, take our strength take our will, Never shall the evil raise never ever it will. Now hear our prayer. We call the Mother Nature the supreme to grant the old queen power".

Suddenly the twister exploded and there stood a tall slim beautiful doe eyed woman her hair was black her fingers were lean as reed. Her bosoms blossomed like lotus flower. She wore a full sleeved fan collared magenta colored gown.

She walked to the man who resurrected her and touched his cheek. Suddenly she felt a flow of memories and remembered everything "Thank you…Amos" said the woman "Your welcome My lady…Hail Queen Ismira" said Amos "Now the battle of good and evil shall begin" said Ismira and walked back to the ashes and touched the leftover ash. Suddenly from the ashes arose a staff, on its top was a structure like claws which held a crystal ball, Ismira pulled out the staff and waved her hand over it. The ball glowed seeing which she cackled with laughter.

Flairs and Glairs, a platform by a student for the students. We are esteemed youth struggling to carve out our path for our future and we follow a basic mindset Since everyone is not born with all-round skills. Joining hands with people who are born to execute it with perfection is the best way to evolve. Self-Evolution is the need of the hour but, evolving as a community is what we strive for. The initiative as kickstarted by, Founder- Mr. Shubham Shah with the motive to utilize the skillset and talent of writing has now a team of 10+ people who are actively participating into newer forms of learning and discovering talents among youngsters. We Provide platform and services like Publishing opportunities, Open mics, Workshops, Hands-on training. Operating with Brand Name of Flairs and Glairs (Publication House), we offer the chance of elevating a passionate writer to an esteemed author With Brand name Teekhe Zasbaaat. We bring to you an opportunity to get accustomed with the Public Speaking and Presenting of Thoughts along with regular challenges to brush up your inking spirit. The newest initiative to extend our services we introduced in a new writing Platform- The Glittering Fables and Ink Over Tears.

We Choose to Fly Like A Falcon than to be a Leg Pulling Crab.

To Know More: Infoline – 7781900870

Mail Us At-

flairsandglairs@gmail.com / info@flairsandglairs.in

Or Visit is at

www.flairsandglairs.com / www.flairsandglairs.in

Social Handles- @flairsandglairs @teekhezasbaaat